This book is loved by

This book is dedicated to all the little MONKeYs in the universe, but especially to my favorite MONKeYs: Jonathan, Eleanor and Katie

Written and illustrated by Suzanne Kaufman

COMPENDIUM™
INCORPORATED

MONKEY wanted to be something special.

MONKeY tried to be a bUNny, but it was too Floppy.

MONKeY tried to be an **elephant,** but it was too **wrinkly.**

MONKEY tried
to be a Squirrel, but
it was too nutty.

MONKeY tried to be a cUCUMBeR, but it was way too cool.

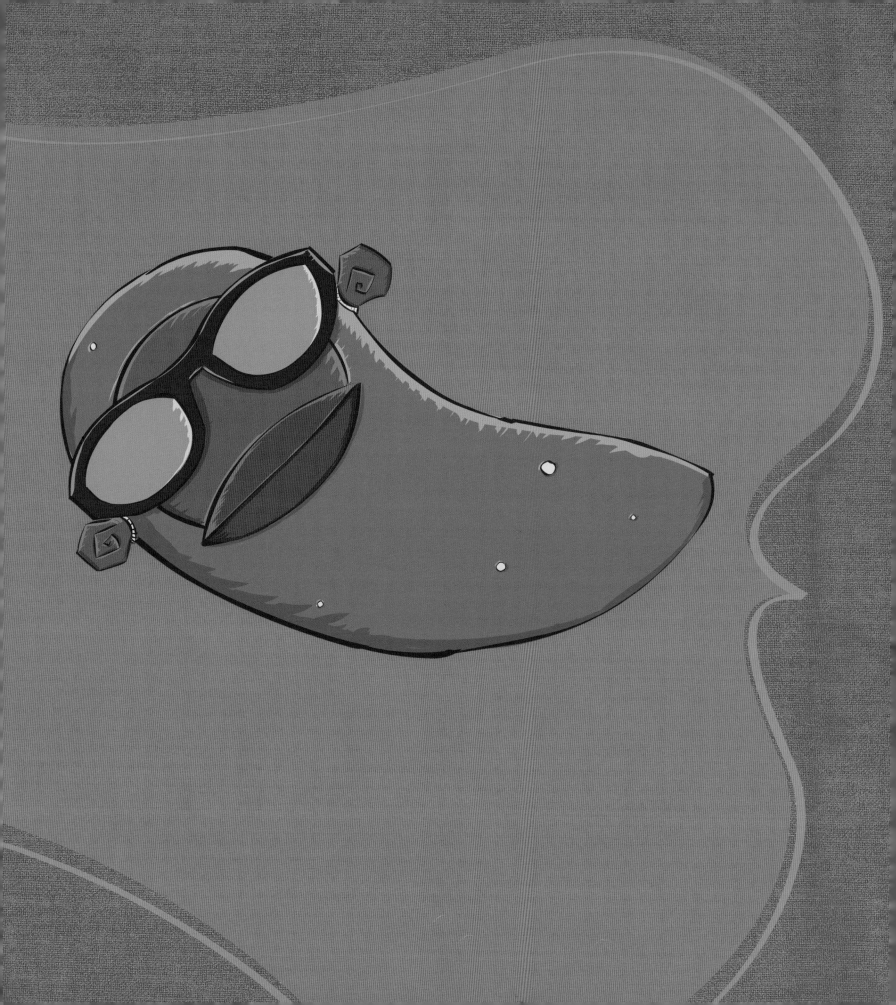

MONKEY tried to be a chicken, but it was quite clucky.

MONKeY tried
to be sushi, but it
was too tasty.

MONKeY tried to
be a **MONSteR,** but that
was just too **ScaRy.**

MONKeY tried to be a penguin, but it was too frosty.

MONKEY tried to be a **bee,** but it was too **bumbly.**

MONKeY tried to
be a night owl, but
it was too sleepy.

MONKeY tried to be a **vegetable,** but it was too **CoRny.**

MONKeY tried to be the **solar System**, but it was just too vast.

Then one day MoNKeY
had a WONDeRful thought:

"Maybe I can't be a buNNy,
or an elephant, or a SquiRRel.
But there's one Very special thing
that I can be—I can be mySelf!
No one in the entire world can
ever do a better job of being me
than me. And that makes me special.
That makes me...a snuggable,
lovable, one-of-a-kind
MoNKeY!"

Written and illustrated by
Lil MoNkey

Edited by
DaNo

Co-edited by
Kristel ChaNdelier

Designed by
SarahRaMa

Inspired by
The KoBester

Published by
COMPendium, Inc.

In loving memory of Charles Kaufman, who lived life like every day was Sunday.

To Mom and Dad: Thanks for the extra crayons, boxes, tape and glue, and for buying me the first monkey that set me down this path.

To my amazing husband, Jonathan: Thank you so much for believing in me all the way (and for letting me sleep in on Saturdays to catch up).

To Eleanor and Katie, my wonderful daughters: Yes, you have lots of monkey in you, and I love it!

To the German Club: Thanks for all your support, coffee, feedback and giggles. Thanks Sondra, Paul, Andy, Jeff, Priscilla and Kirsten. Special thanks for the great late-night talks, Sondra, and the crazy lunch dates, Paul. You two are amazing.

To my publisher, Compendium: You guys rock! This book was so fun to make with you. Thank you for all the silly, wonderful collaboration, ideas, support and feedback. Without you there would be no "I Love Monkey."

To Kobi Yamada: Thank you, Kobi, for laughing and giggling with me, for believing in this wonderful, wacky character, and for helping me find my own inner monkey.

To Sarah Forster, my amazing designer: If I could thank you with an Elaine dance, I would. You always bring that magical funk and style that helps everything fit together and makes me want to jump for joy.

To Dan Zadra and Kristel Wills, my editors: You guys are toooo great. Thanks for loving Monkey as much as I do. And thanks for helping me put such heartfelt words to this quite crazy but wonderful idea. You made this book come alive.

Library of Congress Control Number: 2009928261

CREDITS

Written and illustrated by Suzanne Kaufman
Edited by Dan Zadra & Kristel Wills
Designed by Sarah Forster

ISBN: 978-1-932319-52-1

3rd Printing. Printed in China with soy ink. A011006003